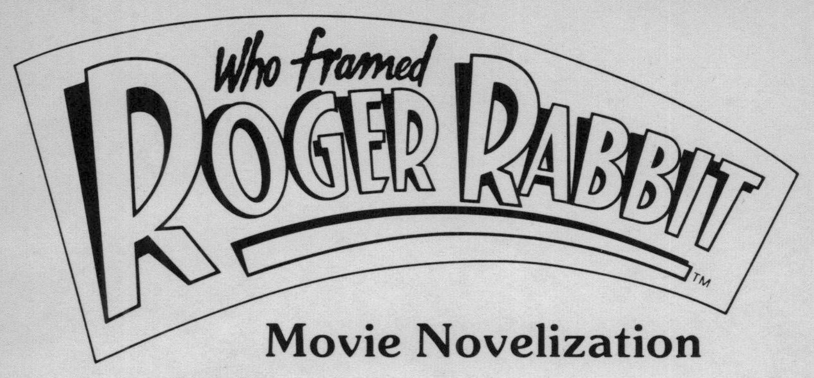

Movie Novelization

Based on the hit motion picture from
Touchstone Pictures and Steven Spielberg

Executive Producers
STEVEN SPIELBERG and KATHLEEN KENNEDY
Produced by
ROBERT WATTS and FRANK MARSHALL
Screenplay by
JEFFREY PRICE and PETER SEAMAN
Directed by
ROBERT ZEMECKIS
Novelization adapted by
JUSTINE K

A GOLDEN BOO
Western Publishing Company, Inc., Racine,

Chapter 1

"Rabbit sees stars! Not birds, *stars*!" the director shrieked at Roger Rabbit. A ring of cartoon birds flew around Roger's head. Roger Rabbit, the star of countless Maroon Cartoons, was in a daze.

"Huh?" Roger murmured absentmindedly.

Roger wasn't distracted because a refrigerator had been dropped on his head. He was a Toon, and Toons could take anything. Toons could get squashed flat by a steamroller, then fill themselves up with air and get up again, good as new. They could float in a soap bubble or slide under a closed door or slip through a keyhole. Like the great movie stars of Hollywood, Toons had a special magic and the power to make an audience laugh or cry or simply forget their troubles.

Offscreen, however, Toons could have troubles of their own, just like anyone else. And today Roger Rabbit was having a hard time forgetting about his troubles. It was affecting his work.

Roger plucked a tweeting bird from the flock circling his head. Why couldn't he come up with stars? He'd done it before. In fact, Roger was a big success because he always did exactly what the director and the audience wanted.

But today Roger's heart, like his attention, was far

from Maroon Cartoon Studio. Roger was heart-broken because of his sweetheart, Jessica.

"I'm a lovesick loon, a loony Toon, a harebrained hare, to think that a gorgeous Toon like Jessica could really love a silly rabbit like me," Roger mumbled.

"Take five," the director shouted.

"I can give you stars," Roger pleaded with the director. "Don't worry about dropping the refrigerator on me. I can take it."

"I'm not worried about you," the director explained. "I'm worried about the refrigerator."

"I can give you stars," Roger pleaded. "Watch."

Roger banged himself on the head with a frying pan. Exclamation points sprang from his head, then a cuckoo clock, but no stars.

From the back of the soundstage private detective Eddie Valiant watched the zany rabbit disgustedly. "Toons," he thought. "I've had enough of them to last a lifetime."

He jiggled pennies in the pocket of his worn trench coat. It was all the money he had in the world. Maybe this case would change that. Maybe he could get back on his feet. When his brother, Teddy, was alive, Eddie had been half of the greatest detective team in town. With Teddy gone, Eddie had lost confidence in himself, and he wondered whether he still had what it took to solve tough cases.

Eddie found the office of the studio head, R.K. Maroon. He walked past the blond receptionist and into R.K. Maroon's office. R.K. leaned over the shoulder of an editor working on a Movieola machine. They were putting the finishing touches on one of Roger's movies.

"Wait until Roger gets to his feet, then hit him with the boulder," Maroon told the editor.

The editor nodded, snipping bits of film and splicing them together on the machine.

"Get a load of this scene, Valiant," R.K. said when he saw Eddie.

Eddie watched the film clip. It was part of Roger Rabbit's latest cartoon, *The Bunnysitter,* which also featured another Maroon Cartoon star, Baby Herman, a short tough-talking fifty-year-old Toon who always played a mischievous baby.

"Whew!" Maroon sighed, wiping tears of laughter from his eyes. Then he looked over at the unsmiling detective. "Boy, what a stone face. I hope whatever you've got isn't contagious, or I'll be out of business."

"Are you paying me to laugh, or do you have a case for me?" Eddie snapped.

R.K. raised an eyebrow but quickly explained the situation. "I'm $25,000 over budget on the latest

Baby Herman cartoon. You saw the rabbit blowing his lines. He can't keep his mind on his work."

Maroon tossed a copy of the *Toontown Tattler* onto Valiant's lap. Eddie scanned the front-page article. "Jessica, the girlfriend of Maroon Cartoon star Roger Rabbit, was seen breaking breadsticks with an unidentified gentleman with lots of cash. Hare today, gone tomorrow? This column wonders if Roger and Jessica's days together are numbered."

Valiant threw the paper back to Maroon.

"What's this got to do with me?" he asked.

"Roger's all torn up about this gossip. Jessica is nothing but trouble, but he thinks she's an angel. I want you to follow Jessica and get some pictures of her with this sugar daddy. Once the rabbit's wised up, he can get back to work. I've got a picture to finish!" Maroon shouted.

"I don't work Toontown," Eddie stated.

"What's wrong with Toontown?" Maroon asked. "Everyone and his brother loves Toontown."

"Then get everyone and his brother to do the job," Valiant said. He shuddered at just the thought of working in Toontown.

"Relax. Nobody said you had to go to Toontown, anyway. Jessica sings at a place called the Ink and Paint Club. It's a Toon revue, but the audience is strictly human," Maroon explained.

Eddie stared out the window at the strange characters who filled the studio backlot. An alligator in a soldier's uniform marched past a fairy princess and a frog buying a meal at a lunch stand. Workmen unloaded wooden crates stamped Gag Beartraps, Gag Rockets, Gag Slingshots. They dropped a crate labeled Gag Musical Chairs, and a bunch of Toon chairs playing musical instruments tumbled out, blaring jazz as frantic workmen tried to round them up.

"Well?" Maroon asked.

It looked as if Eddie had sunk to the lowest rung in the private detective business, being a Peeping Tom for Toons.

"It'll cost you a hundred bucks, plus expenses," Valiant declared.

"That's ridiculous!" R.K. protested.

"So's the job."

Chapter 2

Eddie searched his pockets. Without three more cents, he wouldn't be able to get on the trolley—at least not in the usual way. He couldn't afford the fare, so Eddie sneaked onto the back of the Red Car Trolley as it moved down the street.

"Don't you have a car, mister?" asked a dirty-faced kid hanging beside Eddie.

"Who needs a car? This city has the best public transportation in the world," Valiant replied.

As they sped past the trolley terminal Eddie pointed to the billboard on its roof proclaiming, "Los Angeles' Pacific and Electric Red Car—America's Finest Public Transportation System." Eddie noticed workmen with ladders, buckets, and brushes on the roof near the sign, but the trolley turned the corner before Eddie could see what they were doing.

The workmen were pasting a sign over the Red Car billboard, a white sign emblazoned with a bright green four-leaf clover.

The smell of stale french fries and yesterday's onions greeted Valiant as he pushed inside the Terminal Cafe. Dolores, the waitress, looked up from behind the counter. Her heart fluttered when she saw Eddie.

"Hey, Dolores," Valiant said, sitting on one of the

empty stools. He pulled Maroon's check out of his pocket and slid it across the counter. "Put this toward what I owe you."

Dolores studied the check, then whistled softly. "R.K. Maroon, as in Maroon Cartoons?"

"Who's your client?" asked huge, hulking Angelo, a man only slightly smarter than his cheeseburger. "Screwy Squirrel hire you? Does Little Bo Peep need help finding her sheep?"

Dolores glared at Angelo. "Knock it off."

As long as Eddie had a job, she didn't care who had hired him. Embarrassed, Eddie glanced around the restaurant.

"Earl?" he called to a sad man hunched at the end of the counter. Eddie barely recognized Earl without his Red Car Trolley uniform. "What's with you? Shouldn't you be working?"

Earl stared silently at his french fries.

"He got laid off," replied Sarge, the seedy old soldier who sat two stools down from Earl. "A new outfit bought Red Car. Some big company called Cloverleaf."

For a moment no one said anything. Eddie could hear Angelo chewing his burger and the coffeepot boiling over. Then a trolley car clanged past, and Earl sighed.

As Dolores poured catsup from a nearly empty

bottle into a full one, she thought, "This place is so gloomy it isn't a Terminal Cafe, it's a terminal disease."

"Can I borrow your camera, Dolores?" Eddie asked. "Mine's in the shop."

"As in pawn shop?" Dolores said.

"I need it for the job," Eddie explained. "When I'm finished, I'll pay you the rest of the money I owe you."

Dolores reached under the counter and produced a camera. There was some film in it.

"Thanks," Valiant said. He shoved the camera into the pocket of his trench coat and walked out of the café.

The camera was still in Eddie's pocket when he stepped past the hairy bouncer of the Ink and Paint Club. The customers were all human, but the bouncer was a big Toon gorilla. The bartender was a Toon octopus who was busy shaking, stirring, and pouring with all eight arms at once. The waiters were Toon penguins dressed in tuxedos.

Onstage, two Toon ducks took turns upstaging one another during a piano duet. The crowd howled with laughter. Eddie scowled and found an empty table next to a garishly dressed man whose laughter was even louder than the colors of his plaid suit. He was slapping his knees and roaring with laughter as he tried to sign his check. He was shaking a fountain pen that stubbornly would not produce any ink.

When Eddie leaned over to offer his pen, the man's fountain pen squirted ink all over Eddie's shirt. Now the man was really laughing!

"You think that's funny?" Valiant asked, staring down at the ink spot on his shirt.

"It's a panic," the man said, gasping with giggles.

"Let's see you laugh at this," Eddie said, waving his fist in the man's face.

"Calm down, son," the man said, placing a plaid-clad arm around Eddie's shoulders. "Look. The stain's gone already. It's disappearing ink."

Eddie looked at his suddenly spotless shirt.

"No hard feelings," the man said, shaking Eddie's hand vigorously.

An electric shock buzzed up Eddie's arm like a platoon of army ants.

Howling with laughter, the man managed to gasp, "I'm . . . Marvin . . ."

"The Gag King," Valiant muttered to himself. He knew about Marvin from the *Toontown Tattler.* Marvin had bought Toontown with the money he had made selling gags and novelties to cartoon studios.

"Isn't it a gasser?" Marvin asked as he showed Eddie the hand buzzer concealed in his palm. "These are our number-one sellers."

"Nothing like the classics," Eddie growled, rubbing his arm.

The lights dimmed, and a hush fell over the crowd.

"I never miss a night when Jessica's singing," Marvin said, sitting up straight. He rubbed his hands together and leaned forward with anticipation.

A spotlight hit the curtain. Whistles and cheers drowned out the beginning of the smokey blues song the band was playing as Jessica stepped into the spotlight.

Eddie loosened his shirt collar, which suddenly felt tight. Jessica was a Toon, all right, but she was the most beautiful Toon Eddie had ever seen. Eddie, like the other customers, was entranced.

Marvin reached over to close Eddie's mouth.

"*She's* married to Roger Rabbit?" Eddie said with a gasp as Jessica began singing.

By the time Jessica sat on Eddie's lap for the finale, he was ready to grow rabbit ears and a cotton tail. He barely heard the applause as she looked deep into his eyes and whispered, "Thanks for the lap."

Jessica jumped up and was gone before Eddie could recover his senses. Then he saw Marvin head backstage with a bouquet of flowers. Eddie ran to follow him.

He saw Jessica open the dressing room door and Marvin step eagerly inside. Eddie looked over his shoulder before crouching to peek through the keyhole. So far all Jessica had done was put the flowers in water. Marvin was talking and . . .

A furry hand grabbed Valiant's shoulder.

"Whaddya think you're doing, chump?" grunted the gorilla bouncer.

"Who are you calling a chump, chimp?" Valiant asked. The bouncer responded by tossing Eddie out the club's back door.

Eddie found himself in an alley behind the club.

"I've been thrown out of better joints than this," he called to the gorilla. Then, as he brushed the dirt off his coat, he muttered that he'd also been thrown out of worse joints.

Eddie reached into his pocket for the camera. He climbed on a crate and peered into the window. There was Marvin, knee-to-knee with Jessica in earnest conversation. Valiant snapped the pictures until he ran out of film.

Later that night Eddie brought the pictures to R.K. Maroon's office. Roger Rabbit was already there.

Roger ranted like a mad March hare. "I don't believe it. I won't believe it. I can't believe it. I shan't believe it. I . . ."

"Believe it, you crazy Toon," Valiant said angrily. "I took the pictures myself."

Roger sobbed. His thin white shoulders shook and big Toon tears sprang from his eyes. "But, Jessy! She's the light of my life, the apple of my eye, the cream in my coffee . . ."

"Well, you better start drinking it black. It looks like Marvin's her man now," Eddie snapped.

"I thought he was my friend," Roger said.

"It's hard to believe," R.K. agreed. "Marvin's been my friend and neighbor for thirty years."

"You're better off without her," Valiant told Roger. "A good-looking guy like you can always find someone else."

Roger couldn't believe what he was hearing. He was furious. His ears flew straight up in the air and steam shot out of them with a deafening whistle. Roger's eyes popped out of his head as he leapt onto Maroon's desk and grabbed Eddie by the lapels.

"Someone else? There's only one woman in the world for me!" Roger shrieked wildly.

Then he jumped off the desk and crashed through the window, leaving a rabbit-shaped hole.

Eddie looked at Roger's silhouette in the window. He sighed and said, "At least he took it well."

Chapter 3

Every time Eddie opened the door to his office, a flood of painful memories swept over him.

On the frosted glass in the door were the words *Valiant and Valiant, Private Investigation.* There was a picture of a knight on a white horse below the letters.

Inside the office, Eddie looked at his brother Teddy's empty chair, the double desk they used to share, and the walls covered with pictures taken during their days together as "Toontown heroes."

Those were the good old days, days when Eddie knew how to laugh—days when he used to take off his shoes before he fell asleep. Those days were gone forever, or so it seemed. Eddie sat down at his desk. Feeling tired, he leaned back and closed his eyes. Soon he drifted off to sleep.

Eddie's dreams were interrupted by the crash of his metal wastebasket on the linoleum floor. He raised his head and came face-to-face with Lieutenant Santino of the Los Angeles Police Department.

"Santino! Where'd you come from?" Valiant grumbled.

"Holy cow, Eddie! If you needed money so much, why didn't you come to me?" Santino said.

"So I took a few pictures," Eddie said. "So what?"

"Thanks to your amateur photography, I've got a stiff on my hands," the lieutenant growled. "Marvin the Gag King is dead. The rabbit dropped a safe on him last night."

"Clumsy," Eddie commented.

"*Jealous* is more like it. Get your hat. You've got some explaining to do," Santino barked.

The scene of the crime buzzed with busy policemen dusting for fingerprints and searching for clues amid the cartoon clutter in Marvin's Gag Factory. Two white-coated men from the Coroner's office ran after some Squeaking Toon Shoes that had escaped from a spilled crate. A couple of reporters on the scene played with Toon mallets that had spring-loaded boxing gloves inside them.

"It's just like a Toon to drop a safe on a guy's head," grumbled Santino. Then, noticing Valiant, he muttered, "Sorry, Eddie."

Valiant shrugged his shoulders and followed Santino to the chalk outline the police had drawn around Marvin's body. The gray metal safe was wide open, but before Eddie could look inside, one of the detectives slammed it shut. The detective grabbed the rope that was dangling from the factory ceiling. He scraped off a sample of yellow paint and carefully dropped it into an envelope.

"What's that?" Valiant asked.

"Paint from the cartoon rabbit's glove," the detective replied. "Not that it's any of your business."

Valiant rubbed his chin. "Something about this case stinks," he thought. "Why is everyone so sure the rabbit is guilty?"

Eddie smelled an intoxicating perfume and heard a sultry voice call his name. He turned to see Jessica, who slapped his face so hard he got whiplash.

He was still reeling from it when two men shuffled past carrying a stretcher. Eddie could see a plaid-clad arm sticking out from under a sheet. A hand buzzer clattered to the floor.

Eddie reached for it, but he found his hand pinned by the end of a cane. He looked up past the cane's gavel-shaped head, past a long stretch of black pants and a black robe, to the vulturelike face of Judge Doom. Above the huge hooked nose were rimless tinted glasses whose lenses gave Doom's face a skull-like appearance.

"Is this man removing evidence from the scene of the crime?" Doom thundered.

"Uh . . . no, Your Honor. Valiant was just picking it up for you. Weren't you, Eddie?" Lieutenant Santino said.

Eddie stared at Santino and the judge. Who was

this creep? Santino was that polite only to the Police Commissioner, or maybe his mother.

Doom extended a gloved hand toward Valiant and commanded, "Hand it over."

Eddie suppressed a grin as he pressed the buzzer into Doom's hand with an electrifying BUZZ. Eddie almost heard Marvin's ghost laugh as he added, "It was his number-one seller."

Doom's hand vanished in the folds of his black robe, and he sneered, "I see working for Toons has rubbed off on you."

Eddie's face flushed with anger as he protested, "I don't work for Toons. I was hired by R.K. Maroon."

"We spoke with Mr. Maroon. He told us the rabbit became agitated when he saw your pictures. Tell me where the rabbit is and I might stop considering you an accessory to murder," Doom said.

"How should I know where the hare hopped?" Eddie snapped. "And who are you, anyway?"

Santino tugged Valiant's sleeve and made a face. But Doom only laughed.

"I am The Law," he replied. "And now that Toontown is under my jurisdiction, I intend to make Toons respect that law."

"This guy is as batty as Carlsbad Caverns," Eddie thought. Just then a paddy wagon emblazoned with

"Los Angeles Police Dept. Toon Squad" screeched to a halt outside. A group of sinister Toon weasels popped from its doors and stood cleaning their fingernails with switchblade knives and polishing their guns. At a signal from Doom, two rolled a 20-gallon metal drum out of the wagon and pried off the lid.

"I'll catch the rabbit, Mr. Valiant, with or without your help," the judge announced. "Then I'll try him, convict him, and execute him."

A Squeaking Toon Shoe bounced past Doom's glossy black shoes and was captured in a swift sweep of Doom's gloved hand. Doom threw the shoe into the vat, where it melted to oblivion in mid squeak.

"What is that stuff?" Eddie whispered to Santino.

"Remember how we thought there was no way to kill a Toon?" Santino whispered.

Eddie nodded.

"Well, that stuff does the trick. Turpentine, benzene, acetone, paint remover . . . it kills Toons," Santino went on. "He calls it the Dip."

Doom reached into the vat with a rubber-gloved hand, then held a test tube up to the light as if inspecting a fine wine.

"Needs more benzene," he told the head weasel, who rushed to do Doom's bidding.

"How did this gargoyle ever get to be a judge?" Eddie whispered into Santino's ear.

"He spread a lot of money around Toontown," Santino said nervously. "Bought the election."

Doom pointed a paint-stained, gloved hand at Eddie. "These aren't kid gloves, Mr. Valiant. This is how we handle difficult Toons. I should think you'd appreciate that. After all," he added, "wasn't your brother killed by a Toon?"

Halfway up the stairs to his office, Eddie knew he wasn't alone. The smell of cheap perfume emanated from the landing where a tall blond woman leaned over a baby carriage. When Eddie reached the door, Baby Herman stuck his head out of the carriage and asked, "Are you Valiant?"

"Sometimes," Eddie replied.

"Listen. I want to talk to you about Marvin's murder," Baby Herman said. "The rabbit didn't kill Marvin. Roger may be a loony Toon, but he's not a murderer. I should know. The idiot's a dear friend of mine."

"Tell it to Judge Doom," Valiant said wearily. "As far as he's concerned, Roger's his man. I mean, rabbit."

"All he has is circumstantial evidence," Baby Herman went on. "This whole thing stinks."

Baby Herman pulled a newspaper from his carriage, tossed it to Eddie, and continued talking.

"The paper says Marvin left no will. That's a load of succotash. Every Toon knows Marvin had a will. He promised to leave Toontown to us Toons. That will is the reason he got bumped off. Someone had other plans for Toontown."

"Anyone ever see this will?" Eddie asked.

"No. But Marvin gave us his solemn oath," Herman asserted.

"That joker couldn't do anything solemn," Valiant replied, pushing past Baby Herman to open his office door. "The joke's on you."

"I thought since you were the one who got my pal in trouble, you might want to help him," Baby Herman said. "I can pay you."

Valiant shoved the carriage away from his door. And as the Toon star rolled down the hall, Eddie told him, "Save your money for elevator shoes."

Inside his office, Valiant muttered to himself, "It isn't my fault the rabbit got himself in trouble. All I did was take some pictures."

He tossed Baby Herman's paper onto the desk and used it as a pillow.

"For a guy who's got a bed, I sure do a lot of sleeping at this desk," Eddie said with a yawn.

With the front page pressed against his cheek, Valiant noticed something he hadn't seen before. He sat upright and opened a desk drawer. He began sifting through the contents—mostly paper napkins and coffee stirrers—until he found his magnifying glass. He wiped the dust off it and held the glass above the newspaper blowup of the photo he had taken of Marvin and Jessica in her dressing room.

"Bingo!" Eddie exclaimed.

A piece of paper was sticking out of Marvin's pocket. On it were the blurred-but-legible words *Last Will and Testament of Marvin the Gag King.*

"A will is not something you carry around every day," Valiant mused. "Marvin must have known something was up. . . ."

Eddie felt the old thrill of the chase, that surge of adrenaline the hound gets when he smells the fox. It was the same feeling he and Teddy had shared when they found the first big clue that marked the beginning of an exciting new case.

Eddie looked across the desk at Teddy's empty chair, then walked wearily to the Murphy bed against the far wall. He pulled down the bed, determined to sleep off the crazy notion of getting involved in a lousy Toon case.

"Aw, the heck with it," Eddie said with a sigh, dropping onto the bed.

Then he screamed.

Chapter 4

Roger Rabbit screamed, too.

For a moment the detective and the Toon rabbit stared at each other, nose to twitching nose on the bed. Eddie recovered his voice first. "How did you get in here?!"

"Through the mail slot," Roger replied. "I thought it'd be better if I waited inside, considering I'm wanted for murder."

"That was considerate, but did it ever occur to you that I might not appreciate being arrested for aiding and abetting a criminal?" Valiant retorted, grabbing the rabbit by the ears and dragging him to the door.

"But I'm innocent!" Roger protested. "Sure, I wanted to win Jessy back, but not that way."

When Eddie tried to open the door, Roger stretched his arms and legs across it like a spider clinging to its web in the wind.

"After I left you and Maroon, I went to see Jessica at the Ink and Paint Club," he explained.

Valiant gave up on the door and pulled the rabbit instead.

"She was onstage, so I wrote her a love letter."

Roger snapped off the frame like a broken rubber band, sending the two of them tumbling backward.

Eddie stood and brushed himself off, then looked at Roger skeptically.

"You mean in a jealous rage you went and wrote Jessica a love letter? I suppose you used lipstick on the mirror," Eddie sneered.

"Lipstick, yes . . . mirror, no. I found a nice clean piece of paper in her dressing room," Roger said, pulling a lipstick-scrawled page from his pocket. "Dear Jessica," he read. "How do I love thee? Let me count the ways. 1-1000, 2-1000, 3-1000 . . ."

Before Roger could reach 4-1000, Eddie snatched him by the ears, threw him out the door, and slammed it hard.

"7-1000, 8-1000 . . ." Roger recited as he slid back in through the mail slot. "Obviously a love letter of such power and sensitivity must be read in person. So I went home to wait for Jessica. But the weasels were waiting for me, so I ran."

"If you're innocent, why did you run?" Eddie asked.

"Well . . . I'm a rabbit," Roger replied.

Eddie had to admit he had a point. Besides, all along he'd had a hunch the rabbit was innocent. But that didn't mean that he, Eddie Valiant, was going to get mixed up in some loony Toon case.

"Get out and stay out, or I'm calling the cops," Eddie growled, grabbing the telephone.

"Go ahead—call the cops," Roger huffed. "I come here for help, and what do you do? You turn me in. Thanks for nothing!"

And with that, he stalked to the door, threw it open with a flourish, and slammed it behind him.

"That's the closet," Valiant said with a sigh.

When there was no response, Eddie opened the door and found Roger Rabbit dressed in his trench coat and hat. Playfully Roger snapped one end of a set of handcuffs on Eddie's wrist and the other on his own.

"Eddie Valiant, you're under arrest!" Roger exclaimed. Then, seeing Eddie's face darken with rage, the rabbit quickly added, "Just kidding."

"You idiot!" Valiant said angrily. "I lost the key to those cuffs."

Tires screeched outside. Roger ran to the window, dragging Eddie with him.

"It's the Toon Patrol!" Roger shrieked. Toon weasels poured out of the paddy wagon, carrying butterfly nets and Toon violin cases.

"Get outa here!" Eddie groaned.

"You've got to hide me!" Roger pleaded.

Valiant tugged at the cuffs and nodded. "I've got better things to do than wait for a locksmith in Doom's Toon tank."

Weasels silhouetted in the frosted glass demanded, "Open up in the name of the law!"

Eddie looked around the room frantically. "What would Teddy have done at a time like this? He would have panicked," Eddie thought. Eddie was doing that just fine on his own.

The weasels gave up knocking and started pounding. "Don't make us play rough, Valiant. We just want the rabbit."

Since he was already white, Roger turned pea-green with fear.

"This rabbit couldn't murder a marshmallow," Eddie thought. "But Marvin sure didn't drop a safe on himself, so who . . ."

"You've been forewarned!" a weasel shouted before blasting the door with a burst of machine-gun fire. Suddenly there was a huge hole in the door. The weasels stepped warily into the empty office, then followed the sound of Eddie's whistling to the bathroom. Guns ready, they flung open the door.

Valiant turned to them over a sink full of suds and said coolly, "Hello, boys. Didn't hear you come in."

Weasels swarmed all over the bathroom, checking behind the toilet and shower curtain.

"All right, where's the rabbit?" the chief weasel demanded.

"You mean the rabbit with the orange pants, buck

teeth, big floppy ears, and clodhopper feet?" Eddie asked.

"Yeah," the weasel snapped impatiently.

"Haven't seen him," Valiant replied.

The chief weasel regarded the soapy water suspiciously and asked, "What's in there?"

"My underwear," Eddie answered, pulling a dripping sock from the suds and throwing it onto the towel rack.

"Search the place, boys," the chief weasel commanded. "And leave no stone unturned!"

While the weasels tore up the office, Valiant pulled his other hand out of the water, the one with the cuff. A soapy, blue-faced rabbit came gasping to the surface. Eddie covered the sound with a yawn, exclaiming, "Wash day is so tedious."

"Look, Valiant, we got a reliable tip that the rabbit was here. And it was corroborated by several others. So cut the &%$#@!" shouted the chief weasel.

"If you keep talking like that, I'm going to have to wash out your mouth," Eddie said primly, jamming a bar of soap into the weasel's mouth.

The Toon weasel gagged and coughed up a stream of soap bubbles. His fellow weasels wheezed and gasped with laughter.

The chief weasel spat out the soap and commanded the other weasels to stop laughing. But more bubbles popped out with each word, and the weasels only laughed harder. The chief weasel grabbed the toilet plunger, stuck it on the snout of the nearest weasel, and warned, "You know what happens when you can't stop laughing!"

The weasels exchanged nervous glances and immediately stopped laughing. As they were leaving, the weasel said, "Step out of line, Valiant, and we'll hang you out to dry with your laundry."

As soon as the door slammed shut, Roger shot out of the water and gave Eddie a big wet Toon kiss.

"Aw, Eddie, you saved my life! How can I ever repay you?" Roger asked breathlessly.

Valiant wiped his mouth disgustedly. "For starters, don't ever kiss me again."

At the Terminal Cafe, Dolores was listening to the radio, dreamily humming along with the music.

Suddenly the program was interrupted by a news bulletin.

"Newsflash . . . . Hollywood. Citywide Toonhunt for Roger Rabbit, suspect in the slaying of Marvin the Gag King. Police describe him as cute, cuddly . . . and psychotic."

When the café door swung open, the down-and-out regulars all turned at once to look at the new arrival. It was Eddie, with the squirming bulge of Roger Rabbit in his trench coat.

"Hey, Eddie—you made the front page today," Sarge called. He waved the paper at Eddie.

"I read it," Eddie snapped, brushing past Angelo and walking toward Dolores. He took his hand out of his pocket and shook the handcuffs. "I need to get out of these," he whispered to Dolores.

She raised an eyebrow and stepped out from behind the counter and walked to the back of the restaurant. Dolores turned a broken light fixture sideways, and a wall panel rotated to reveal a secret back room.

Inside the musty room were cases of catsup, mops and cleaning supplies, broken chairs, tools, and other assorted junk. While Dolores looked for a hacksaw, Roger sprang from Eddie's coat and explored his surroundings. He discovered a peephole that looked into the café. Sarge's lips moved as he read his newspaper, while unhappy Earl complained to his coffee cup, "Twenty years working for Red Car Trolley, and now this . . ."

"I thought you said you'd never take another Toon case. Have a change of heart?" Dolores asked, handing Eddie a hacksaw.

"Nothing's changed," Eddie grumbled. "Somebody made a patsy out of me and I'm gonna find out why. If I let Doom have Roger, this case will be closed faster than you can say 'turpentine.' "

Valiant sawed feverishly at the cuffs, then barked at Roger, "Hold still! You're blocking my light."

Roger quietly slipped his paw out of the cuffs and stepped out of the light.

"Better?" he asked from across the room.

"Yeah," Eddie muttered, sawing a few more strokes before it hit him. He looked up.

"You mean you could have taken your hand out of those cuffs anytime?!" Eddie demanded.

"No," Roger said. "Only when it was funny."

If Valiant had been a Toon, steam would have hissed out of his ears. Luckily he wasn't a Toon.

"Is he always this funny, or is it only when he's wanted for murder?" Dolores asked sarcastically.

"My philosophy is, if you don't have a sense of humor, you're better off dead," Roger explained.

"You may have your wish, unless I find out what happened to Marvin's will," Valiant said.

"What will?" Dolores asked. "Fill me in."

"Baby Herman told me that Marvin was going to leave Toontown to the Toons," Eddie began. "But the way I figure it, Marvin's neighbor, R.K. Maroon, wanted to turn Toontown into Maroontown. So he hatched a plan with Jessica to bump off Marvin, frame the rabbit, and destroy the will."

"Jessica would never—" Roger began.

"That's perfect!" Dolores interrupted.

"Except for one thing," Eddie elaborated. "I don't think they got the will. This morning I noticed Marvin's safe was still open. You could drop one of those from Mt. Everest and it wouldn't open. Somebody went to the trouble of cracking it, and my guess is they came up empty-handed."

Dolores smiled. Here was the old Eddie Valiant, the guy she'd fallen in love with so long ago.

"Anything I can do?" Dolores asked.

"Yeah," Eddie said. "Better check probate court. See what the word is on Marvin's estate."

Dolores nodded. "You think Maroon's going to bid on the property?"

"That's my hunch," Eddie replied. "Oh, and one more thing. Can Roger stay here?"

"He's not going to do anything crazy, is he?" Dolores asked.

She and Eddie turned to the rabbit, who had taken a file from the toolbox and stuck it through one ear and out the other. With a look of ecstasy on his face, Roger dragged the file back and forth, as if scratching his brain. Before she could answer, Eddie kissed Dolores and was gone.

Chapter 5

Once again Eddie dragged a crate under the window of Jessica's dressing room. "No pictures this time," he thought as he smashed the window. Tinkling glass shattered the silence in the alley. Valiant waited tensely to see if anyone had heard the noise. Then he opened the latch and pulled himself through the window.

Eddie flicked on his flashlight and scanned the room. Wherever it had ended up, Marvin's will had been in this room the night before. Valiant rifled the drawers of Jessica's dresser but found nothing. Then, in the wastebasket, under Marvin's wilted flowers, Eddie spied a blue piece of paper. It was the cover of a legal document.

"Last Will and Testament—Marvin the Gag King," Valiant read. Then he felt a hard blow on his head, and he blacked out.

When he came to, Valiant rubbed his eyes and realized it wasn't a dream. The gorilla bouncer of the Ink and Paint Club was exhaling banana breath in his face, while Doom, his weasels, and Jessica glared down at Eddie.

"Rummaging around a lady's dressing room," said Doom with a frown. "What were you looking for?"

Roger Rabbit was always popping up in odd places like Eddie Valiant's closet.

To make sure Eddie would help him, Roger slipped a pair of handcuffs on the detective's wrist.

The weasels of the Toon Patrol struck fear in the hearts of all the Toons in Toontown.

Eddie hid Roger in his coat when he went to the Terminal Cafe.

Judge Doom was the most powerful man in Toontown, and he was determined to catch Roger Rabbit.

Roger Rabbit sneaked through the Gag Factory's plumbing and burst out of the drainage grate to challenge Doom.

Doom flicked a switch and a ton of cartoon bricks fell on poor Roger Rabbit.

Judge Doom met his doom in a terrible liquid called the Dip.

"You know very well," Valiant said, looking at Jessica. "I was looking for Marvin's will."

"Marvin had no will," Doom replied. "I should know. The estate is in my jurisdiction."

"He had a will, all right. She and R.K. Maroon killed him for it. Then she double-crossed him," Eddie went on, pointing a finger at Jessica.

"You have the wrong idea about me, Mr. Valiant," Jessica said. "I'm not really bad—I was just drawn this way."

"You've expressed some imaginative allegations," Doom hissed at Valiant. "Do you have proof?"

"Not yet," Eddie conceded.

"And no sign of your imaginary will?" Doom asked with just a trace of a smile.

"I found the cover it came in," replied Eddie. He reached into his pocket, but the blue envelope was gone. "They must have taken it," he said.

"They?" Doom asked.

"Someone else was here looking for Marvin's will," said Eddie.

"Don't worry about this supposed will," said Doom. "We'll handle this our way—the Toon way."

As he strolled back to the Terminal Cafe, Eddie realized that he was racking up quite a criminal record on this case: accessory to murder, harboring a fugitive, breaking and entering . . . just like the good old days. And even if he hadn't found the will, Valiant felt he was getting close to the answers. He waved to Dolores, who was approaching the café from the other end of the street.

"What's the word, hummingbird?" Eddie crooned.

"Maroon isn't after Toontown like you thought. It's Cloverleaf. They put in the highest bid," Dolores said. Then she pointed to the new sign that covered the Red Car billboard on the roof of the trolley terminal and proclaimed, "Cloverleaf . . . for a Smooth Ride into the Future."

"And unless the will shows up by midnight tonight, Cloverleaf will own Toontown," she added.

Eddie stared at the bright green four-leaf clover and mused, "First they buy the Red Car, now they're after Toontown. I don't get it."

"Listen. Is that music coming from the Terminal Cafe?" Dolores asked.

Eddie heard faint sounds of honky-tonk music and singing. He exclaimed, "Roger!"

Valiant and Dolores raced to the restaurant and found Roger entertaining the regulars with his own special song-and-dance routine. The zany rabbit made up words as he went along, working his way down the line of frowning faces, teasing and tumbling, until he coaxed a smile out of each one, even Earl.

Valiant grabbed Roger by the ears, threw him into the back room, and scolded him. "Why, you crazy Toon! I've been out risking my neck for you, and you're singing and dancing?"

"It's my calling," Roger replied. "My purpose, my reason for living. Toons are supposed to make people laugh. And those people needed some laughs."

"Will you be laughing when they turn you in to the cops?" Eddie demanded. "That bum Angelo would rat on you for a nickel."

"He's my pal," Roger protested.

"Because you made him laugh?" Eddie scoffed.

"Laughter can be a powerful thing," Roger said. "Sometimes it's the only weapon we have in life."

Valiant's hands were clenched in furious fists.

Before the argument could go any further, a red light flashed over the door. Eddie threw Roger on the floor and rushed to the peephole. He could see Judge Doom and his weasels standing in the doorway of the café.

"I'm looking for a murderer," Doom announced, holding out a gloved hand at counter height. "A Toon rabbit, about so high."

"There's no rabbit in here," Dolores said defiantly. "So don't harass my customers."

"I didn't come here to harass," Doom answered sweetly, "I came to reward."

He stepped to the blackboard that listed the day's specials, and where it said, "Cheese Dip—$.50" he wrote, "Rabbit Dip." A hush fell over the crowd when Doom replaced the "$.50" with "$5,000."

"Hey, I've seen a rabbit," Angelo volunteered.

Eddie turned to Roger. His look said, "I told you so."

"A rabbit with orange pants, buck teeth, big floppy ears, and clodhopper feet," Angelo continued.

"Where?!" Doom shouted impatiently.

"In the movies. He's funny," Angelo said.

The Terminal regulars burst out laughing, while Doom fumed. He stared at them menacingly until the laughter died down. Silence gripped the room, except for the grating sound of a record player stuck at the end of a record.

Judge Doom whirled around and grabbed the record off the player. He read the label triumphantly, "The Merry-Go-Round Broke Down." Then Doom declared, "Quite a loony selection for a bunch of bums like you. The rabbit is here. I know it!"

Doom sailed the record across the room right into a weasel's mouth. The other weasels laughed wildly until Doom silenced them with a nasty look. The weasels then produced Toon crowbars, sledgehammers, and picks.

"Do you want to tear the place apart?" the chief weasel asked.

"That won't be necessary," Doom said with a sneer. "The rabbit will come to me."

Judge Doom rapped his gloved knuckles on the counter in a familiar rhythm. "Da da-da da dum . . ."

"Shave and a haircut . . ." Dolores thought as she recognized the rhythm of the knocking.

Doom walked around the restaurant tapping the rhythm on tables, walls, and closet doors. He cackled and said, "No Toon can resist the old shave-and-a-haircut trick."

Valiant watched Doom through the peephole. "I don't know who's crazier, Doom or you," he said to Roger. But when he looked at Roger, he saw that the rabbit's knees were shaking and he was sweating heavily. There was fear in Roger's eyes.

"Da da-da da dum . . ." The knocking came nearer. Roger bit his fingernails and now his knees were knocking. Roger started moving toward the secret door. An unseen force was pulling him and he couldn't resist it.

"Don't do it," Valiant hissed, making a desperate grab for Roger's ears.

Doom had reached the false panel in the back wall. "Shave . . . and . . . a haircut . . ." he said loudly.

Roger streaked past Eddie. He crashed through the wall and shouted the rest of the jingle. "Two bits!"

Doom smiled and grabbed Roger. He held Roger's ears firmly and grinned at Eddie through the rabbit-shaped hole in the wall.

"Arrest that man!" he ordered his weasels, who eagerly stepped forward to grab Valiant.

"He didn't have anything to do with this, Your Honor," Roger told Doom earnestly. "He never even aided me. He never abetted me. He doesn't even know me. Let him go."

Doom chuckled. "We'll see to Valiant later. Right now I'm in the mood for an execution."

Two weasels scurried obediently out the door.

"Hey, this is America," Earl protested. "The rabbit's got rights."

"What about his trial?" Angelo demanded.

Doom snapped his fingers. The chief weasel handed him a briefcase and announced, "Oyez . . . oyez. Court is now in session."

Doom opened the briefcase and twelve Toon kangaroos popped out, neatly arranged in a jury box. As the Terminal regulars stared in stunned silence,

Doom rapped his gavel-headed cane on Roger's skull to begin the trial.

"The defendant is charged with the cold-blooded murder of a human, Marvin the Gag King. How do you find the defendant?" Doom asked the jury.

Twelve baby kangaroos popped out of their mothers' pouches, each holding a letter to spell Y-O-U A-R-E G-U-I-L-T-Y.

"Guilty as charged," Doom concluded, snapping the briefcase shut. "Case closed."

On cue, the two weasels returned with a steel tub filled with a sloshing green liquid.

"For this terrible crime, I sentence you to the Dip!" Doom declared, dangling Roger above the tub.

"Doesn't the prisoner get a last request?" Valiant asked, looking for any way to delay Roger's demise.

"It's only right that a condemned man get a last meal," Dolores added. Roger shot Doom a pleading and hungry look.

"I'm feeling generous today," Doom said, "so go ahead. But make it short." Turning to the weasels, he said, "Keep an eye on the rabbit."

Roger sat down at the counter, and Dolores served up the day's special, a big plate of spaghetti and meatballs. Despite the seriousness of the situation, Roger couldn't resist making a little joke.

"It's a shame things have come to this," Roger said, "but that's the way the meatball bounces." Roger picked up a meatball and bounced it on the counter. The weasels began giggling. "Weasels laugh at anything," Roger thought. Then he had an idea.

"I love spaghetti," Roger exclaimed as he dumped the whole plate of pasta on his head. The weasels began to laugh harder. Roger took his plate and smashed it on his head. The weasels laughed wildly.

"Silence, fools," Doom warned, but the weasels couldn't control themselves. Roger grabbed a pile of plates and jumped on the counter. He began smashing the plates on his head. The weasels were now rolling on the floor, holding their sides as they convulsed with laughter.

Roger looked at Eddie and said, "I hate to eat and run, but . . ." Eddie realized what Roger was up to and made his move. He grabbed Roger by the ears and kicked over the tub of Dip. The weasels, and even Doom, recoiled in horror from the hissing green liquid spreading across the floor.

Eddie and Roger ran out of the café and dived into the front seat of the Toon paddy wagon.

"There's no key!" Valiant exclaimed desperately.

Just then, Eddie and Roger heard a deep voice from the back of the paddy wagon.

"Hey, you weasels! Let me outa here! I have to make a living!"

"Benny!" Roger exclaimed, recognizing the voice of the Toon cab locked in the back of the paddy wagon.

"Open the back, Eddie," Roger said, jumping out of the wagon. "We've got a ride!"

Chapter 6

Eddie pried off the paddy wagon's lock to the cheers of a comical assortment of captive Toons, who quickly made their escape.

"Nice going," Benny told Roger, winking one headlight. "Who's the human?"

"Eddie Valiant, meet Benny the Cab. Benny, meet Eddie," Roger replied cordially.

"Can we speed things up?" Valiant urged as he and Roger jumped into Benny's backseat. "Get us out of here," Eddie shouted.

Benny's grill was twisted into a mischievous smile. He revved his engine and sped down the street. Angry weasels coughed in a cloud of Toon dust as they piled into their paddy wagon.

At the end of the street Benny's path was blocked by a streetcar. Tires squealing, Benny braked suddenly and spun around 180 degrees. The Toon wagon struggled to follow. Eddie clutched the dashboard as Benny zoomed through traffic, performing stunts that most Toon cars wouldn't dare.

"We've lost the weasels," Roger shouted.

"And we've gained two Los Angeles Police Department motorcycles," Eddie yelled over the roar of Benny's engine.

"By the way, Benny, what were you in the Toon paddy wagon for?" Roger asked.

"Reckless driving," Benny replied as he squeezed between two speeding trucks. "Do you believe it?"

"Hard to imagine," Eddie said. Then he shouted in Roger's ear, "If we live through this, I'm going to kill you."

Suddenly the Toon squad wagon barreled down an alley straight at Benny. With the police motorcycles roaring behind him, there seemed to be nowhere to go.

"Pull the lever!" Benny commanded.

Roger did, and at the last possible moment the Toon suspension on the cab shot up and stretched like an accordion. Benny sailed right over the furious weasels.

"Weasels, meet motorcycles. Motorcycles, meet weasels," Roger recited to the sound of screeching tires and crashing motorcycles behind them.

Eddie's legs were still shaking when he stepped out of the Toon cab in front of the movie theater.

"Thanks for the ride," Roger said. "Let's do it again real soon."

Valiant grabbed Roger by the ears and stuffed him into his hat.

"We're going to lay low for a while," Eddie grumbled as he bought a ticket.

Eddie found a pay phone in the lobby of the theater. He called Dolores and told her where he and Roger were.

"Can I borrow your car?" Eddie asked her. When Dolores said yes, Eddie asked her to leave it outside the theater with the keys in it.

Inside the dark theater, people were watching a cartoon. Valiant sat in the empty back row of the balcony. He took off his hat and told Roger to keep quiet. But Roger was soon laughing so loudly that people were turning around in their seats.

"We're supposed to be in hiding," Valiant scolded. "What's wrong with you?"

"What's wrong with you? You're the only person in this theater who isn't laughing," Roger replied. "What could have happened to you that turned you into such a sourpuss? What could be so bad that—"

"You really want to know?" Eddie asked. He was at the end of his patience. "A Toon killed my brother."

"A Toon?" Roger asked, incredulous.

"We were investigating a robbery of the First National Bank of Toontown. Back then Teddy and I liked working Toontown. There were always lots of laughs. Anyway, we trailed this guy to a place on Yockster Street. We went in; he got the drop on us. Literally."

Roger winced. "A safe?"

"Piano. It broke my arm. Teddy didn't make it," Eddie answered.

"Who was the Toon?" Roger asked gently.

Eddie shrugged. "I don't know. All I remember is him standing over me, laughing, with those burning red eyes. He disappeared into Toontown. I finally gave up looking. That's the story. Are you happy now?"

Roger sobbed. "That's terrible! Now I know why you hate me so much. If a Toon killed my brother, I'd hate me, too."

"Stop crying," Eddie said. "I don't hate you."

"Yes, you do, or you wouldn't have yanked my ears," Roger said with a sniffle.

"I'm sorry I yanked your ears, OK?"

"All the times you yanked my ears?" Roger persisted.

"Yeah . . . all the times I yanked your ears."

Roger's ears lifted and a smile lit his silly face. "Thanks, Eddie. I feel better now."

Roger extended his paw, and they shook on it. Just then the cartoon ended and the newsreel came on.

"In California," the announcer said, "Cloverleaf Oil was on the move this week, buying two important Hollywood companies, the Red Car Trolley and Maroon Cartoon Studio."

On the screen, R.K. Maroon happily displayed a check for $3.5 million. Eddie nearly jumped out of his seat. Roger stared at him, confused. Eddie got up and Roger quickly followed.

"I had it all wrong," Valiant explained as he worked his way through the lobby to the phone. "I thought Maroon wanted to buy Marvin's land. What he really wanted was to sell his own. But Cloverleaf wanted Maroon Studio, plus Marvin's Gag Factory. It had to be a package deal or Cloverleaf wouldn't buy."

Roger scratched his ears.

"R.K. Maroon, please," Eddie yelled into the phone, then with his hand over the receiver he said to Roger, "If R.K. wants his 3.5 million, he's going to have to sweat for it."

Eddie told R.K. he had Marvin's will, and they arranged to meet. Then Eddie and Roger left the theater. They found Dolores's car out front, got in, and headed for the Maroon Studio.

By the time they reached the deserted studio, Roger had broken into a cold sweat. His knees knocked together, his buck teeth chattered, and he fretted, "Maroon might get mad when he finds out you don't have Marvin's will."

"Just cover my back," Valiant snapped, slamming the car door.

Roger flung himself onto Eddie's back, clinging to his coat until the detective peeled him off. "I mean stay here while I get some answers."

Roger paced in front of the car nervously and muttered, "My jaw's set, my ear's to the ground, my eyes are peeled. No one gets the drop on me!"

Suddenly a Toon frying pan came down on Roger's skull with a resounding bong. Roger was out cold. His body was dragged off and dumped into the trunk of a nearby car.

Meanwhile, R.K. and Eddie enjoyed a lively discussion in Maroon's plush office.

"Have you got the will?" R.K. demanded.

"Sure," Eddie lied. "The question is, have you got the way? It isn't going to come cheap."

"OK, hardcase. How much?" Maroon snapped.

"Let's see. Your take was 3.5 million . . ." Eddie began.

"Don't get the wrong idea," Maroon protested. "I was going broke. I had to sell. I'd never have done it if I knew what they were planning. I can still stop it, if you give me the will."

"What plan?" Eddie asked coolly.

R.K. shot him a suspicious glance. "Show me the will. I want to see it now."

"Fancy talk for a murderer," Valiant retorted.

"I'm a cartoon maker, not a murderer," Maroon

declared. "Sure, I was desperate. Maroon Studio was failing and I had a chance to sell to Cloverleaf. But they were only buying if Marvin sold his Gag Factory, too."

Eddie yawned and said, "Tell me something new."

"I thought I could persuade Marvin to sell if I came up with some incriminating photographs of him and Jessica. Jessica was willing to help, because I told her I'd fire Roger if she didn't," Maroon added.

Valiant scratched his head thoughtfully. "Let's pretend I believe you. What's Cloverleaf going to do with the land? Drill for oil?" Eddie asked.

"It's worse than that. Cloverleaf is out to destroy Toontown, and all the Toons," Maroon said, his eyes darting anxiously around the room. "And unless the will shows up by midnight tonight, Toontown is going to be a free—"

R.K. froze in mid sentence as a dozen Toon weasels popped out of hiding places all around his office. Suddenly Maroon vanished, leaving Eddie to dive for the door and wonder, "Free . . . free what?! Free lunch? There's no such thing. Land of the free and home of the depraved?" As the weasels searched the office Eddie ran down the hall.

Outside, Eddie discovered that things were just as

confusing. Roger was nowhere in sight. Eddie spotted Jessica's car speeding out of the parking lot. Eddie jumped into Dolores's car, floored the gas pedal, and drove off in pursuit.

Valiant's stomach knotted in fear as Jessica's car raced into the Toontown tunnel. He chased Jessica through streets he hadn't seen since he and Teddy had walked them together. Jessica finally stopped and got out of her car. She glanced over her shoulder and started down the street.

Meanwhile, Roger had come to and found himself in the trunk of Jessica's car. He began screaming, "Let me out!" Eddie heard Roger and released him from the trunk. Then he handcuffed the groggy rabbit to the steering wheel of Dolores's car.

"Why the cuffs, Eddie?" Roger asked.

"I'm going after Jessica. She's into this up to her pretty neck, and I don't want you to be confused about who's your pal," Eddie said.

Before Roger could speak, Valiant ran after Jessica. He followed her through what seemed like an endless dark maze of Toontown alleys and back streets. Just when he thought he'd lost her, Eddie heard a noise and turned around, bumping into Jessica's back. They both screamed.

"You've been wrong about me, Valiant," Jessica said when she'd caught her breath.

"So I keep hearing. Let's start with why you bonked the bunny and work backward from there."

"I was afraid Roger would get hurt," Jessica explained. "I knew he wouldn't come with me willingly, and the studio was crawling with weasels out to get him. It was Doom who killed Marvin."

"Why didn't you tell me that before?"

"I didn't know if I could trust you," Jessica said. "Marvin wasn't sure who was with Doom. He was awfully scared that night in my dressing room. That's why he brought me his will."

"Where is the will?" Valiant asked.

Jessica shrugged her beautiful shoulders. "When I opened the blue envelope, the only thing inside was a blank piece of paper."

"Marvin was a joker to the end," Eddie thought.

"Let's go back. I'm worried about Roger," Jessica urged. But when they got back to the spot where Dolores's car had been, all that was left was a crumpled bumper. Jessica groaned, "That's what you get for leaving Roger alone with a car. He loves to joyride."

"At a time like this?" Eddie exclaimed, suddenly noticing that they were surrounded by weasels.

Chapter 7

Valiant looked from one mob of evil-looking weasels to another. Luckily for Eddie, Benny the Cab screeched up that very second. "Need a lift?" he asked.

Jessica and Eddie jumped in, and Benny sped toward the Toontown tunnel. Unknown to Benny, a dark figure waited in the tunnel with a giant steel drum. A well-polished black shoe kicked over the drum to spill a slick of Dip into Benny's path.

Benny skidded when he hit the hissing liquid. His rear tires smoked, then evaporated. He squealed out of control and crashed into a streetlamp. Benny's headlights went out. The brave Toon cab was knocked out.

Eddie and Jessica were hurled from the cab onto the roadway. The Toon Patrol wagon screamed into the tunnel, and weasels popped out and surrounded them.

"What an unfortunate accident," Doom purred from the shadows. "Don't just stand there, help them," he told the weasels.

"No, thanks. We'll wait for the Automobile Club," Eddie joked.

"Oh, no . . . I insist you ride with me!" Doom protested. "You'll enjoy attending our ribbon cutting at the Gag Factory." The weasels threw Eddie and Jessica into the wagon and drove off.

A few minutes later Roger drove into the Toontown tunnel in what was left of Dolores's car. Benny winked a headlight and called to Roger.

"Benny?" Roger asked, barely recognizing him.

Benny hobbled over on his axles. When Benny saw Roger's handcuffs, he popped open his trunk and found bolt cutters, and then clipped the rabbit free.

"Doom's got Jessica and Valiant," Benny said. "He took them to Marvin's factory."

"Get Dolores," Roger told Benny. "We're going to need help."

"And you may need this," Benny said. Benny handed Roger a Toon gun. Toon guns couldn't really hurt anyone, but Roger thought it might scare a few of Doom's weasels.

Benny drove away, leaving Roger alone to face Doom, his weasels, and the unknown. The rabbit was afraid, but for a change he didn't run. Roger climbed into Dolores's car and drove off to the Gag Factory.

Inside the factory, two of Doom's weasels held Eddie and Jessica at gunpoint. Some weasels blasted at one of the factory's brick walls with jackhammers, while others rolled a huge drum emblazoned with a skull and crossbones toward a tanker truck. Eddie looked around. What did it mean? Why was all this heavy machinery marked with the Cloverleaf logo?

Behind Eddie and Jessica, several weasels were greedily opening boxes of novelties and gags and stuffing them into their pockets. One of the weasels accidentally tipped over a box of Marvin's Super-Smooth Gag Marbles, and dozens of the marbles spilled out onto the floor. One rolled right under the foot of the chief weasel, who tripped and fell to the floor with a thud. The other weasels laughed loudly.

"Quiet, you idiots," Doom commanded. The weasels instantly fell silent. Doom turned to Eddie and Jessica. "Where is the will?" he demanded.

"I don't have it," Eddie said, "and neither does Jessica. You're out of luck, Doom."

Doom glanced at the factory clock and smiled his evil, thin-lipped smile. "No matter. In fifteen minutes, will or no will, Toontown will legally be mine."

Doom rubbed his gloved hands together, watching his weasels pour the last drum into the tanker truck. Doom adjusted the valves and levers on the truck, then opened a box of gags marked Toon Running Dish and Spoon.

The zany Toon tableware began their merry march. But before the dish had skipped more than two steps, a tanker nozzle hissed a spurt of fluid that erased it on contact. The spoon fled desperately but was hit and reduced to a puddle of ink on the floor.

"Oh, no!" Jessica cried. "It's Dip!"

At that moment brilliant Technicolor Toon light poured in through the hole the weasels had made with their jackhammers. Beyond the hole in the wall stood Toontown. Doom laughed.

"That's right, my dear. Enough Dip to erase Toontown, down to the last tweety bird!" Doom said with glee, pulling the tarp off the truck to reveal several large spray guns.

Roger was peaking through the factory window. Doom's words sent a chill down his spine.

"Dip Toontown?" He gulped. "Well, Roger, looks like you're going to have to bite the bullet, hit the beach, OK the corral." Roger ran to the back of the factory.

"Do you think no one will notice that Toontown has disappeared?" Jessica asked Doom.

"Who will have time to notice what happened to some ridiculous talking Toon mice when they're driving by at seventy-five miles an hour?" he replied.

"What are you talking about? There's no road past Toontown," Jessica exclaimed.

"Not yet!" Doom declared. "Cloverleaf Company is about to embark upon a construction plan of epic proportions. It is called . . . a freeway."

Fireworks went off in Eddie's head. *Doom* was Cloverleaf! Maroon's *free . . .* was a freeway!

"There will be eight lanes of shimmering cement running from here to Pasadena. Smooth, safe, fast. Traffic jams will be a thing of the past," Doom said.

Outside, Roger jammed his thin shoulders against a frosted glass window. He pulled and pulled, but the window wouldn't budge. Exhausted, he leaned against the window to wipe his brow. The window pushed open and Roger tumbled backward, right into the factory washroom.

All the plumbing gave Roger an idea. "Time to plunge ahead," he declared, squeezing his way into the pipes that led down out of the washroom.

Eddie was still facing Judge Doom with anger in his eyes.

"So that's why you killed Marvin? For this freeway?" he demanded. "I don't get it."

"Of course you don't," Doom replied smugly. "You lack vision. But I see a place where people get on and off the freeway. On and off. Off and on. They'll need fuel and food and lodging. Soon, where Toontown once stood, there will be a string of gas stations, motels, restaurants, car dealerships. Cloverleaf gas stations. Cloverleaf motels—"

Eddie interrupted him. "No one's going to take

your lousy freeway when they can ride the Red Car to Pasadena for a nickel."

Doom laughed and said, "They'll drive. They'll have to. I bought the Red Car so I could dismantle it. Soon there will be more freeways crisscrossing all of Los Angeles. That's the way of the future!"

Then he added ominously, "You'll have to take my word for it, because you won't be around to see it."

"Looks like our goose is cooked, our hash is slung, our fait is accompli . . ." Jessica said with a sigh.

"Let me guess where you got that," Eddie said, looking into Jessica's beautiful green eyes. "Tell me. What did you ever see in Roger Rabbit, anyway?"

"He made me laugh," Jessica said, shrugging. "Besides, I love him."

Suddenly Roger exploded out of the drainage grate in the floor. He pointed the Toon gun that Benny had given him at Judge Doom and shouted at the weasels, "Grab some sky, or I let the judge have it!"

The weasels reluctantly raised their paws. The Toon gun had fooled them.

"Roger, darling!" Jessica exclaimed.

"Yes, my dearest. I'd embrace you, but first I have to take care of some unfinished business."

"Put that gun down, you buck-toothed fool!" Doom thundered.

"Go ahead. Give me an excuse to drill ya, ventilate ya, pump ya full of lead!" Roger ranted. "The only thing that can stop me now is a ton of bricks."

"That can be arranged," Doom said as he raised his hand and gave a signal.

A ton of cartoon bricks crashed down from the ceiling onto Roger. A ring of stars danced around the rabbit's head. Valiant looked up to see two weasels snickering in the loft.

"Tie the lovebirds together," Doom said with a sneer.

The weasels tied Roger and Jessica together, then hooked them up to a cable connected to a power winch. Doom hit a button, and Roger and Jessica were hoisted fifteen feet above the floor—right in line with one of the Dipmobile's spray guns.

Doom stepped back to check the line of fire, and suddenly his feet flew out from under him. Doom landed with a crash. He had tripped on the Super-Smooth Gag Marbles the weasels had spilled. He got on his knees and groped for his glasses. The weasels, of course, broke into hysterical laughter.

Eddie's hand moved toward the gun held by the nearest laughing weasel.

"He's going for the gun," Doom shrieked.

The weasel pulled back his weapon. Addressing all the weasels, the judge said, "One of these days you idiots are going to laugh yourselves to death."

"Shall I dispose of him right now, boss?" the weasel with the gun asked.

"Let him watch his Toon friends get Dipped," Doom advised, "then shoot him."

Doom stalked off. The weasels scrambled onto the Dipmobile, started up the engine, and flicked power switches. One climbed to a turret with a spray gun and aimed the gun at Jessica and Roger Rabbit.

"I want you to know I love you, Roger," Jessica cooed.

Roger lifted his chin nobly and observed, "Be comforted in the knowledge that as we face the Grim Dipper, our paint will run together for eternity."

Eddie noticed one of Marvin's jukeboxes behind him. He stepped over to it and hit it with his elbow. Suddenly a nutty song started playing. To the amazement of everyone, especially Roger, Eddie burst out singing. He waddled and wiggled like the looniest Toon, making up rhymes as he went.

"He's lost his mind!" Jessica cried.

"Yeah, isn't it great?" Roger said with delight. "Keep it up, Eddie. You're killing them!"

Roger was right. Laughing hysterically, the weasel

on the turret collapsed onto the trigger, and the cannon sprayed back and forth like a lawn sprinkler. The weasel behind the wheel fell onto the gear shift, and the truck lurched forward. Eddie heaved the last laughing weasel into the discharging Dip. The weasel disappeared with a hiss.

Before Valiant could release Roger and Jessica, Doom used a giant Gag Mousetrap to catapult through the air and land on Eddie's back. Eddie and Doom rolled off the truck, landing separately.

"I never should have let those idiots guard you," Doom hissed with a wicked smile. His cane split to reveal a long, gleaming blade. Eddie reached into a nearby crate, hoping to find something he could use as a weapon. To his surprise he pulled out a sword and yanked it from its scabbard.

"I've got you under my skin . . ." the sword crooned.

Valiant did a double take and looked at the crate. The box was marked Singing Swords. He dropped the Toon sword and reached into a barrel of Toon baseballs. Eddie threw several of them until he realized they were Gag Curveballs. Instead of hitting Doom, they boomeranged back at Eddie.

Jessica and Roger watched the battle helplessly and closed their eyes as the Dipmobile rolled closer and closer. Roger peeked out from behind his ears and sighed. The truck struck a pile of boxes, and the spray gun swung the other way.

Doom advanced toward Eddie, his pale vulture-like face twisted in a hideous imitation of joy. Valiant found a huge Toon magnet, which pulled the blade from Doom's hand with a clang.

Valiant's triumphant smile froze on his lips as he realized the magnet was drawing him inexorably toward a stronger source of attraction, a giant metal Ferris wheel behind him. Soon Eddie found himself clamped to the Ferris wheel by the magnet. Doom laughed as he climbed onto the seat of a Cloverleaf steamroller and drove toward Eddie.

Valiant struggled to lift the powerful magnet, but it wouldn't budge. He glimpsed a box of Marvin's Portable Cartoon Holes and strained to reach it. With the steamroller inches away, Eddie was able to pull a hole from the box and over the magnet. The magnet disappeared into the hole, and Eddie jumped out of the steamroller's path.

The steamroller crashed into the Ferris wheel. Valiant knocked Doom out of the cab. Doom regained his balance and viciously kicked Eddie. Now driverless, the steamroller chugged around in circles.

Valiant used a can of Marvin's Stay-Put Glue as a shield. Doom's foot got jammed in the can, and the judge withdrew a shoe coated with glue. Doom saw the steamroller bearing down on him and realized that his foot was glued to the ground.

Roger flung his ears over his and Jessica's eyes as the steamroller ran over Doom. Eddie climbed the Dipmobile and cut its power seconds before the wildly waving spray could hit Roger and Jessica.

"Eddie, look!" Roger exclaimed.

Valiant turned. Instead of a crushed judge in the steamroller's wake, there was a flat black Doom-shaped pancake. The edges curled up and soon the whole flat figure had peeled itself off the floor and wobbled to its feet.

"Doom's a Toon!" Eddie said with astonishment.

"Surprised?" Doom asked, staggering to a nearby oxygen tank.

"Not really," Valiant said. "That lamebrain freeway idea could only have been cooked up by a Toon."

"Not just any Toon . . ." Doom said.

He stuck the oxygen valve in his mouth and reinflated himself. Doom's glasses cracked and fell to the floor. His teeth shattered out of his mouth like broken china. His fake eyeballs popped out to reveal evil red Toon eyes.

"Remember me, Eddie?" Doom said in a high-pitched voice. "When I killed your brother, Teddy, I talked like this."

Eddie stood paralyzed, just as he had that day, staring into those same hideous red eyes. But this time . . .

Valiant rushed at Doom. The evil Toon turned his fist into an anvil to deliver a bone-crushing punch. Eddie staggered, and Doom slammed him onto Marvin's desk.

With his last ounce of strength, Eddie's hand found the Gag Knockout Mallet the reporters had played with during the investigation of Marvin's murder. He pointed it at the Dipmobile and pulled the trigger. A boxing glove on a giant spring flew across the room and activated a Dip spray gun.

A green flood of Dip gushed over Doom in a deadly wave. As his scream faded, Doom dissolved like a melting candle, and all his evil schemes died with him.

The Toon Patrol, Dolores, and Benny arrived, accompanied by Baby Herman and an assortment of other Toons.

"Eddie, you're hurt!" Dolores exclaimed, seeing a dark stain growing on his shirt.

Valiant stared at the stain. He didn't feel hurt. Then he remembered.

"That's not blood. It's ink. Marvin squirted me the other night. But why is it coming through now?" Eddie wondered.

Roger read the label on a bottle on Marvin's desk. "Disappearing/Reappearing Ink. Gives you enough time to get away from the victim so he doesn't punch you in the nose. Guaranteed to reappear when the coast is clear," Roger read. "What a genius Marvin was," he added.

Baby Herman was angry. "If he was so smart, why didn't he leave his will where we could find it? Toontown is still in danger."

Valiant's face lit up. He had an idea.

"Roger, why don't you read the love letter you wrote Jessica at the Ink and Paint Club that night?"

Roger found the note and began to read, "Dear Jessy . . . How do I love thee? Let me count the . . . I, Marvin the Gag King, being of sound mind and body . . . Hey, it's the will!" Roger shouted.

A crowd of Toons had gathered in the factory. They cheered when they heard the rest of the will. Marvin's will gave Toontown to the Toons in gratitude for all the laughter they had given the world.

"Speaking of laughs," Roger said, "that was some song and dance you did for the weasels, Eddie. Do you think your sourpuss days are over?"

"Only time will tell," Eddie replied.

"Well, put 'er there, pal," said Roger, and he shook Eddie's hand, which was jolted by a tidal wave of tingles. Roger grinned as he held up his hand and showed Eddie the hand buzzer in his palm.

Valiant didn't look amused. He grabbed Roger by the neck. Roger looked scared. Then Eddie gave the rabbit a big noisy kiss. And everyone laughed.

It had been many years since Eddie had enjoyed a good laugh. It felt good, and Eddie got the feeling that if Roger Rabbit had anything to do with it, there would be many more laughs in the future. Suddenly the future looked a lot brighter.